Look! A Book!

Bob Staake

LITTLE, BROWN AND COMPANY

New York   Boston

LO

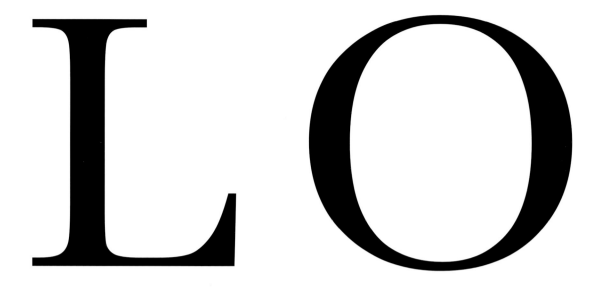

OK!

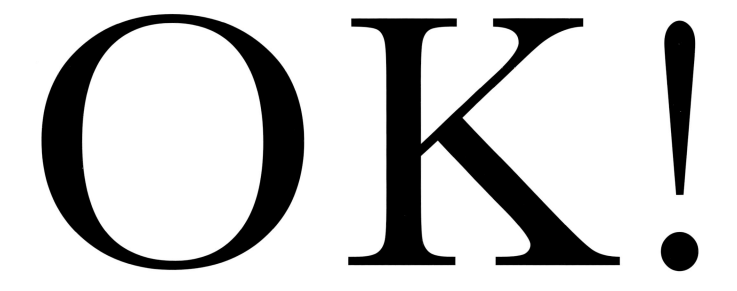

A Book!

HERE'S a CRAZY SEEK & FIND

With images of every kind!

So many objects, big and small. Let's see if you can find them ALL....

Grinning ghosts and pizza planes,

underwater subway trains.

Not a lot of words to read—

the pictures here are all you need!

It's time now to explore this book.

Just turn the page

and take a...

LOOK!

Look!

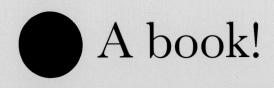 A book!

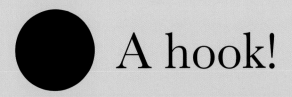 A hook!

A cowboy cook!

Weird and kooky THINGS THAT GO! Some go fast, some go slow!

Can you find the squawking crow?

Look!

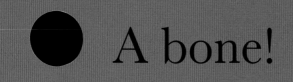 A bone!

A cone! ●

A pumpkin phone! ●

A clock!

A sock!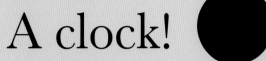

A toothy croc!

MUSEUM CREATURES all escape! Lion! Tiger! Rhino! Ape!

Look and find the vampire's cape!

Look!

● A bowl!

A troll!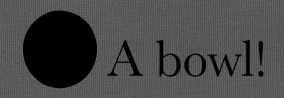

● A barber pole!

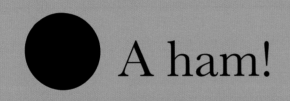 A ham!

A clam!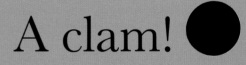

And Uncle Sam!

Bubbles! Bubbles! In the sea! AQUA-GOOFY JUBILEE!

Search to find the honeybee!

Look!

A rake!

A snake!

A slice of cake!

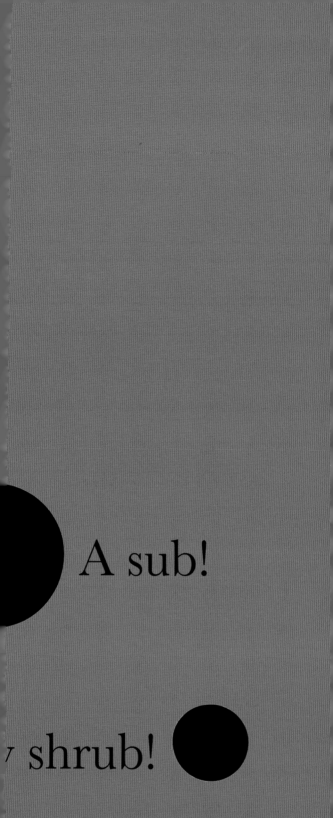

A sub!

shrub!

Lots of fun in MERRYW

Can you find the ice cream swirled?

Look!

A king!

A wing!

A one-eyed thing!

 A kite!

A knight!

A monkey bite!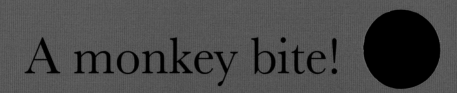

This house is HAUNTED more than most. Too scary for your average ghost!

Quick! Now find the slice of toast!

Look!

A cat!

A bat!

A gooey splat!

A goose!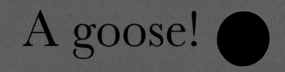

A moose!

A pool of juice!

ROBOTS built here one by one! Bang 'em! Clang 'em! Till they're done.

Can you find the mini one?

Look!

A wheel!

A seal!

A banana peel!

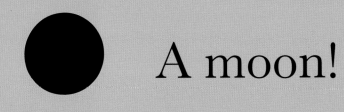 A moon!

A spoon!

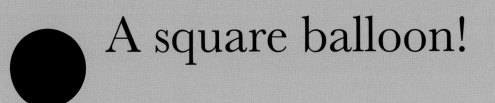 A square balloon!

The kids all love to play around in their crazy TREETOP TOWN!

Look to find the *purr*-fect clown!

Look!

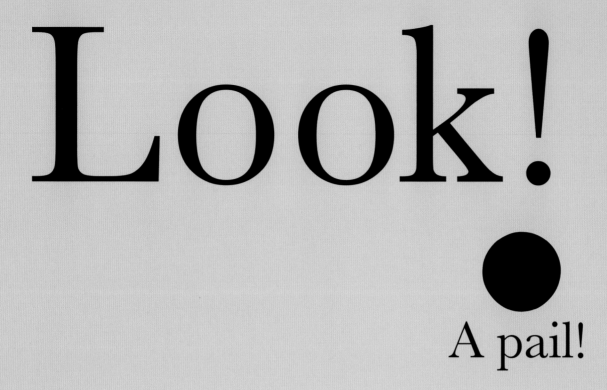

A pail!

A snail!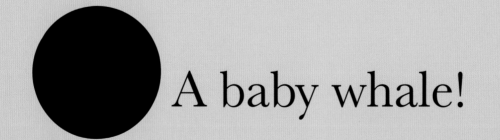

A baby whale!

The End?

No!
No!
No!

STOP!

Just when *you thought* your work was done...

the FUN has only just begun!

Like stinky skunks and chimney sweeps,
dinosaurs and purple sheep!
Toasters, rockets, little frogs,
ice cream-eating wiener dogs!

We hope this book has shown to you
a way to SEE the world anew.
Our journey now comes to an end....

So LOOK again...then TELL a friend!

	F	
1		1
2	O R	2
3	HERMANN	3
4	VON SNE	4
5	LLEN	5
6	B. S.	6

Little, Brown and Company is a division of Hachette Book Group, Inc. • The Little, Brown name and logo are trademarks of Hachette Book Group, Inc. First Edition: February 2011 • ISBN: 978-0-316-11862-0 • IM • 10 9 8 7 6 5 4 3 2 • Printed in China • The illustrations in this book were created by Bob Staake using an old-school mouse, a dusty keyboard, a wood-burning monitor, and an ancient version of Adobe Photoshop 3.0. The text was set in Baskerville. • Book design by Bob Staake and Patti Ann Harris.